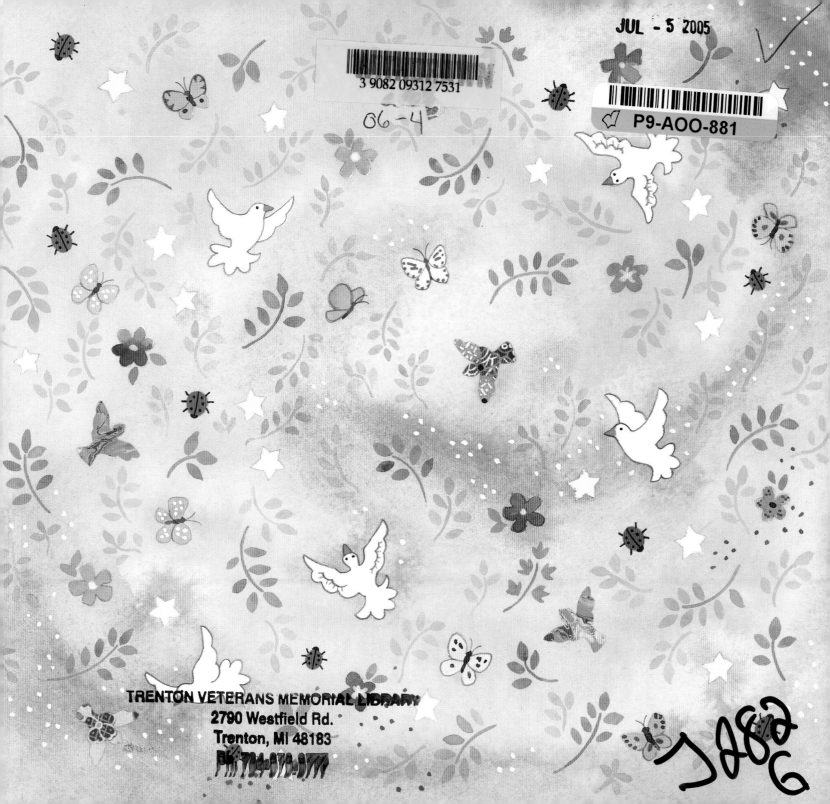

A Peek Into My Church

Wendy Goody and Veronica Kelly

Illustrated by Ginny Pruitt

Los Altos • Pleasanton, CA
United States of America

Nihil Obstat:
Reverend Robert J. McCann, JCL
IMPRIMATUR:
Most Reverend John S. Cummins, DD
Bishop of Oakland
February 28, 1997

To Claudia and Miranda, my whippersnappers — V.K.

To Lauren and Morgan, *my* whippersnappers — W.G.

To Mom, who bought my first box of crayons — G.P.

We would like to extend our thanks to the following people for their very special contributions to this book:

Peter Conaty, Malachy Conway, Herman Leong, Robert McCann, Anni Tervydis & Eleanor Wack. — Wendy & Veronica

Text Copyright © 1997 by Wendy J. Goody and V. Veronica Kelly
Illustrations Copyright © 1997 by Ginny Pruitt

WhipperSnapper Books
1989 Santa Rita Rd. #179
Pleasanton, CA 94566

First Edition
Printed in Singapore
1 3 5 7 9 10 8 6 4 2
Library of Congress Catalog Number 97-060591
Goody, Wendy
Kelly, Veronica
ISBN# 0-9657218-0-9

My name is Liddy (short for Elizabeth Anne Bennett). I have a brother and a sister and my own cat, named Mickey. My family lives in a yellow and white house, and I like to play soccer in my yard with Beth and Roonie, the kids next door.

My family goes to the Catholic Church.

Everyone in our town knows about my church because it is so beautiful. On Sunday, our neighbors and friends fill up the whole church.

We put on nice clothes when we go to church because we are visiting God's house. God loves us a lot and when we go to church we tell God how big our love is. God likes us to visit every Sunday!

I'd really like to take Mickey to church with us, but Mom and Dad say "Pets stay at home."

Why don't you come into my church with me? You will notice right away that it is a special place.

When you walk inside my church, you can see the baptismal font, the seats where we sit during Mass, the altar table, and tall colorful windows made of stained glass. Have you seen these things in your church?

I have a map of a Catholic church to show you. A map is a picture drawn from up above.

To understand my map, imagine that you are a bird flying overhead, looking down at the world. Some maps are pictures of cities and countries. My map shows you what is in my church.

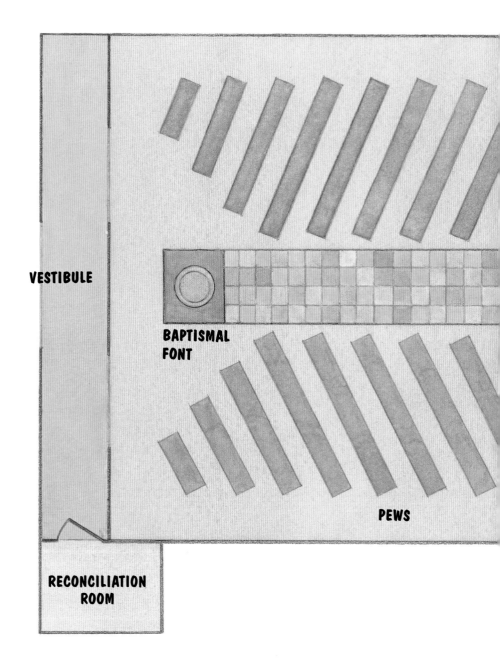

VESTIBULE

BAPTISMAL FONT

PEWS

RECONCILIATION ROOM

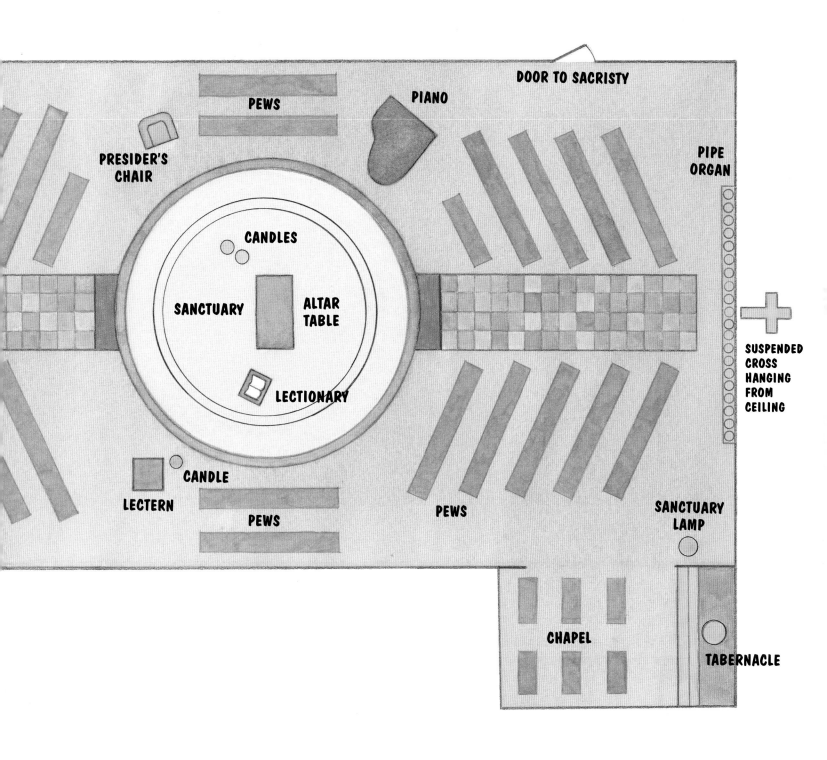

PEWS

DOOR TO SACRISTY

PIANO

PIPE ORGAN

PRESIDER'S CHAIR

CANDLES

SANCTUARY

ALTAR TABLE

LECTIONARY

SUSPENDED CROSS HANGING FROM CEILING

CANDLE

LECTERN

PEWS

PEWS

SANCTUARY LAMP

CHAPEL

TABERNACLE

In my church, the baptismal font is right inside the front door. We use the holy water in the baptismal font to bless ourselves whenever we enter the church.

When I was a baby, I was baptized right here. Do you know where you were baptized? I can't remember being baptized, but Mrs. Rodriquez (she's my godmother) always says that I wiggled like a puppy because the water was so wet.

Now every time I bless myself, I try to imagine being baptized and I think about how my Baptism made me a member of the Catholic Church.

I use my right hand to bless myself with the sign of the cross. First, I gently dip my fingers into the font and then I touch the holy water to my forehead, my heart, my left shoulder and my right shoulder.

If we go right up front and sit in the first row, it's easier to see the altar table. My Mom told me that the area all around the altar table is called the sanctuary. In our church, the sanctuary is a little bit higher than the rest of the church. That way we know where it is.

Mass is celebrated from the altar table and sanctuary. During Mass, Catholics come together to pray and give thanks to God.

When my family arrives for Mass on Sunday, the altar table and sanctuary are quiet. Then an altar server comes in and lights the candles one by one. I love to watch each candle light up.

The people gathering in church and the flickering candles remind me of our special Sunday dinners at home, when we set the table with our best dishes and light candles to welcome our guests.

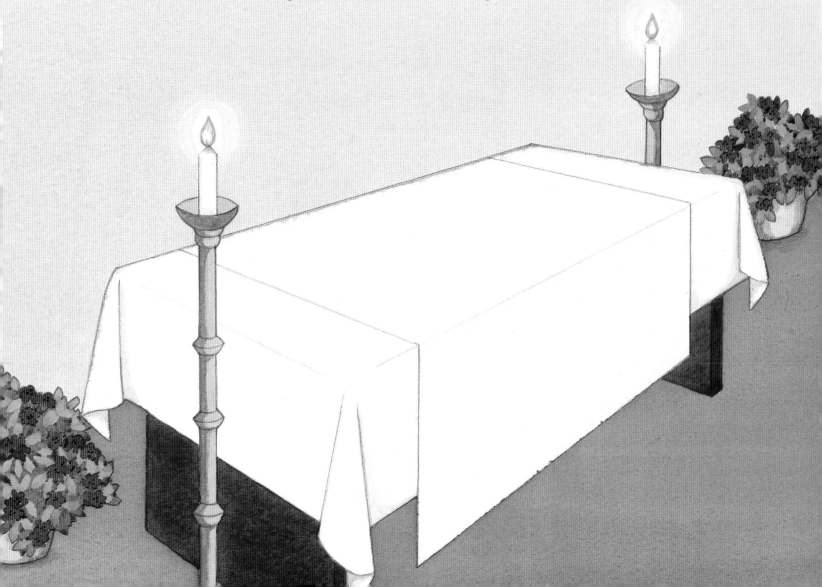

When the choir begins to sing, that's my signal that the first part of the Mass is starting. I stand up as tall as I can to greet our priest, Father Casey, and the church members who walk in with him. I see Roonie and Beth's mom in the procession all the time. She's one of our church readers.

Every Sunday I learn something new from the stories we hear during Mass.

Some of the stories are from the oldest part of the Bible called the Old Testament. Do you remember Noah and his ark? What about Sarah and Abraham? Other stories are from the days when Jesus was alive. These are stories from the New Testament. The Gospel stories in the New Testament tell us about the way Jesus lived his life. On Sunday, the priest gives a talk to help us understand the stories. The talk is called a homily.

Not everything in the Mass is a story. We also say prayers out loud. I'm learning a long prayer called the Apostle's Creed. When I say it, I tell everyone what I believe. I've almost got the whole prayer memorized.

Last Sunday during the Presentation of the Gifts, my family brought the gifts up to the altar table. The Presentation of the Gifts begins the second part of Mass. This is the time when we offer up gifts to God and give thanks for God's love.

Mark and Julia carried the water and wine, Dad carried the collection basket and Mom and I carried the bread. We use the bread and wine for Communion.

Our communion bread is homemade by different families in our church. When my family makes it, we all help sift flour and knead the bread. Mom says "Wash your hands with soap and keep that hair out of your face!"

Communion is the busiest part of Mass. Lots of people get up and go to the front of the church. The church is so busy at Communion time that people wait their turn and go up row by row. After that they go back to their seats and say a prayer.

Mark used to stay in the pew with me and watch Communion, but now he gets to go up with Mom and Dad. That's because he made his First Holy Communion this year. I can't wait for my First Communion.

I asked Mark what Communion is all about.

He told me that every Communion reminds us of the last meal that Jesus ate with his followers. That meal happened the night before Jesus died and it's called the Last Supper.

Mark says that at the Last Supper, Jesus taught his followers how to remember him. He showed them how to take bread and wine from the table and to bless it.

Mark says that Father Casey blesses the bread and wine just the way Jesus did. When the bread and wine are blessed, they become Jesus.

I thought Mark was making this up, but then he told me that God wants us to believe it, even though we can't understand it. The bread and wine don't look like Jesus, but they are!

Father Casey uses a communion plate to pass out the bread and a communion cup to pass out the wine. The cup is also called a chalice (chalice rhymes with palace). You can see them on the altar table during Mass.

Towards the end of Mass, Father Casey puts any remaining bread into the tabernacle. He keeps it there for when someone is sick and needs Communion at home or in the hospital. Then someone from our church can take Communion to them.

At the end of Mass, Father Casey always says "Go in peace to love and serve the Lord."

That's when we all head over to the school for donuts. I always pick the chocolate one with sprinkles, unless Mark gets it first.

I remember that Father Casey came over to my house one day to give my Grandma Bennett Communion when she was sick. He took bread out of a little carrying case that looked like my grandpa's gold pocket watch. Grandma Bennett told me that the case is called a pyx (pyx rhymes with six).

She also told me that Father Casey has many important jobs to do, like celebrating Mass, visiting with people who are sick, saying prayers for families and teaching us how to be good Catholics.

Priests do lots of exciting things, like performing marriages and baptizing babies. Father Casey baptized me! On his days off, he likes to play basketball.

Father Casey calls me Liddy O'Lympic, even though that's not my real name. I see him almost every Thursday night after my gymnastics class. He's eating dinner with some of his friends right next door at Sophie's Italian Restaurant, and we stop to say hello. Sometimes Dad sits down too, and then I can have a soda.

ALB

CASSOCK

ALB with COLLAR

ROMAN COLLAR

SURPLICE

STOLE

Whenever Father Casey celebrates Mass, he gets to wear different clothes called vestments. Mark says that you can always spot a priest when he's wearing his vestments.

Even though I'm still a kid, I know three important parts of the priest's vestments. There's a long white robe called an alb. There's a shorter robe that's like a beautiful poncho and is called a chasuble (rhymes with plausible). Then there's a stole that the priest wears around his neck.

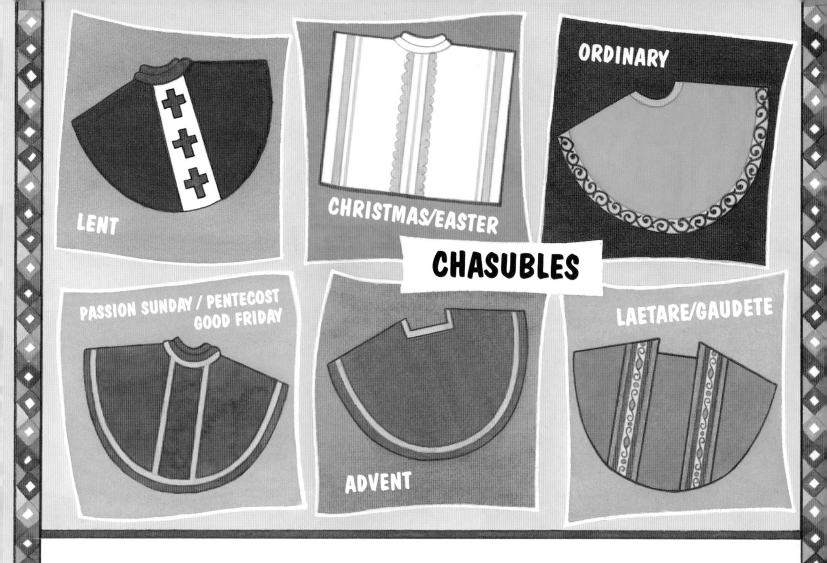

LENT

CHRISTMAS/EASTER

ORDINARY

CHASUBLES

PASSION SUNDAY / PENTECOST GOOD FRIDAY

ADVENT

LAETARE/GAUDETE

When he gave my grandmother Communion at home, Father Casey had on regular clothes. Well, all except his shirt which had a special collar called a roman collar.

But at Mass on Sunday, he always wears his vestments — chasuble, alb and stole. He wears different colored chasubles on different Sundays and each color tells us what Holy Day or season we are celebrating in church.

I like the white and gold chasuble that Father Casey wears on Christmas and Easter the best!

Whenever I have questions about Catholic things I like to ask Sister Carolita. Every Sunday I look around the church to find her and she's always there. She always has a smile for me too!

Sister Carolita isn't like my sister Julia. She doesn't call me poky face or try to eat my potato chips. Sister Carolita is a sister in the Catholic Church.

Sisters are very important people in my church. They do great things for kids and parents too. Wherever you go, you see them working as teachers, as principals in schools and as leaders in hospitals and communities.

Sisters wear clothes that are nice and comfortable to work in. Sister Carolita usually wears a skirt, blouse, jacket and walking shoes. At Mass, she wears her veil too. Sometimes when I see her working around my town, she's dressed just like you and me.

Sisters live and work together just like a family.

In my parish, most of our sisters work in the hospital, but they can work in places all over the world. That's because there are people everywhere who need their help. They feed people who are hungry and try to make sure families are safe and healthy.

There are lots of Catholic families in the United States, where I live. We have Catholic churches and schools all across the country. Look at all the great things that Catholic kids are doing in the U.S. and Canada!

Saskatoon, Saskatchewan
Catholic children celebrate the feast of St. Catherine with La Tire Ste-Catherine, a French Canadian tradition of making pull taffy. They also make Ukrainian Easter eggs, "Pysanky."

Our Lady of Sorrows Elem. School
Vancouver, British Columbia
Students gather in the library once a week to say a rosary together.

Helena, MT
Fifth graders in Helena go to summer camp at Legendary Lodge, a Catholic log cabin retreat.

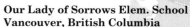

Sacred Heart Elem. School
Red Bluff, CA
Students celebrate Women's History Month by hosting "visits" from these famous women: Wilma Mankiller (Chief of the Cherokee Nation), Maria Mitchell (astronomer), Amelia Earhart (aviator), Beatrix Potter (author), Eleanor Roosevelt (First Lady) and Annie Oakley (sharp shooter). Members of the local women's clubs play the characters.

Red Cloud School
Pine Ridge, SD
The students learn the Lakota language and culture by taking pow wow classes and learning to sing the drum songs.

Our Lady of the Snows Church
Reno, NV
Two young violinists, ages 5 and 6, perform during the Student Mass.

All Saints Elem. School
Hayward, CA
Students bring two lunches to school and donate one to a homeless or poor child.

Queen of Apostles Elem. School
San Jose, CA
Students at this Bay Area school study Earthquake Geology and Marine Ecology with local experts.

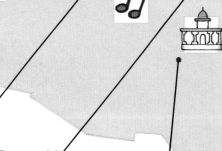

Denver, CO
Denver's Catholic youth help out at The Samaritan House, a local homeless shelter, by donating their time and sharing their toys with the kids staying at the shelter.

St. Elizabeth School
Aiea, Hawaii
Students take hula lessons and perform all over the island.

Madeleine Choir School
Salt Lake City, UT
Every student in this school is a member of the choir. These 4th to 8th grade students have made a CD and cassette of their music and have performed with the Mormon Tabernacle Choir! They sing at Mass every Wednesday and Friday.

Albuquerque, New Mexico
Catholic school children meet with the legislature on "Lobby Day" and present their concerns.

St. Hugo of the Hills
Bloomington Hills, MI
Students rehearse for many weeks each year to produce a spring musical.

"Children Helping Children"
Quebec
On Halloween, children collect money for UNICEF (United Nations Children's Emergency Fund) when they are collecting treats for themselves.

St. Peter's School
Mt. Pearl, Newfoundland
The entire student body participates in the school's annual Skate-a-Thon fundraiser. Blades away!

St. Martha Elem.
Lansing, MI
Students were Grand Prize winners in the 1996 International Schools CyberFair Competition.

École Catholique Cathédrale
Kingston, Ontario
Some students learn their lessons in French (bonjour!), some in English (good morning!).

Buffalo, New York
Children attend the Children's Peace Festival at the Buffalo Zoo.

St Mary's School • Newington, CT
First grade students dress up as their favorite saint on All Saints Day.

Mercymount Country Day • Cumberland, RI
The principal inaugurated National Pull the Plug Week by throwing a very old TV off the roof of the school.

St. Mary's School
Hales Corners, WI
Three 7th graders won regional and state engineering competitions to design a futuristic city.

Holy Child School • Drexel Hill, PA
Students perform MathMagic by doing word problems on the Web.

Philadelphia Archdiocese
Teens publish their own magazine, *Holy Cow*, through the Catholic Standard and Times.

St. Malachy
Creston, IA
This small school of 115 students is proud of their Governor's Scholar and 1st place State Winner of the Daughters of the American Revolution Essay Contest.

Our Lady of the Assumption • Bayonne, NJ
Students met Pope John Paul II at Newark Airport for his Oct. '95 visit to the U.S.

St. Matthew's Elem. • Akron, OH
Children save pop-tops from their soda cans and turn them over to Children's Hospital, where the proceeds buy taxi fares and games for children undergoing dialysis.

Holy Trinity Parish School • Norfolk, VA
During International Week, students are issued passports to travel the globe at Holy Trinity Parish School, where each classroom becomes a different country.

Arkansas
Catholic children from across Arkansas help people hurt by the tornados in 1996 and 1997 by donating food and money.

St. Anthony's School • Covington , KT
Students build bridges from various materials (like pasta!), design golf courses, holocaust quilt squares and even planetary mobiles. Hands on!

Holy Cross Catholic School
Champaign, IL
Students hold a charity basketball game.

Sacred Heart of Jesus • Anniston, AL
The Sacred Heart Scholar's bowl team won top honors at the 1996 Alabama Scholastic Challenge Meet.

New Orleans, LA
Catholic children celebrate Mardi Gras with school parades and celebrations.

St. Mary on the Hill • Augusta, GA
It's no surprise that students on the golf team are working to master their game.

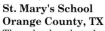

St. Mary's School
Orange County, TX
The school and students are creating a Native Texas Nature Center on the school grounds with trees, shrubs, flowers, bird feeders, birdhouses and squirrel feeders.

Nativity School • Hollywood, FL
Students save their pocket money and donate it to the Make-a-Wish Foundation, which grants wishes to sick children.

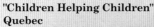
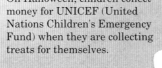

Did you know that Catholic kids live in different countries all over the world? Some live in deserts, some live on mountains and some live beside the ocean. Some even live on islands or in rainforests.

We speak many different languages, but we are all members of the same Catholic Church and we all believe the same things.

I like being a Catholic kid because belonging to a Catholic family makes me happy.

My family does lots of fun things together, like riding bikes and eating popsicles. At home, we always say a prayer before dinner and before we go to sleep. On Sundays we get up early so we are ready for church.

Best of all, Mom and Dad show us how to love each other the way God loves us.

PICTURE DICTIONARY

ABRAHAM and SARAH

In the Old Testament, Abraham is called the "friend of God." He is the founder of the Jewish nation. When Abraham was still childless, God promised him heirs and a land for his people. That land is Israel, where Jesus was born many years later. Sarah, Abraham's wife, bore him a son when he was 100 years old!

ALB

An ankle length, white robe worn under the chasuble.

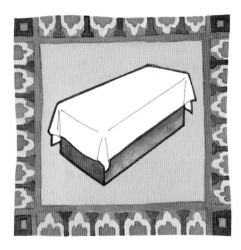

ALTAR TABLE

Catholics think of the altar table as the Lord's table and the people and clergy gather around it for Mass. It is placed at the front or center of the church. A white altar cloth covers the altar table, and a cross and candles are on the table or nearby.

BAPTISMAL FONT

The baptismal font is a basin that holds the holy water used for Baptism. Baptismal fonts are usually located at the front of the church. Sometimes they are in a separate building called a baptistry.

BREAD

Communion bread is unleavened. It is made without yeast, so it does not rise. Bread blessed during Communion is eucharistic bread.

CANDLES

Candles are placed on or near the altar table for the celebration of Mass.

CASSOCK

A full length, tailored robe worn by priests and other clerics, either by itself or under other liturgical robes.

CHALICE

A cup or a goblet, the chalice holds

the wine during Mass. Chalices are made of noble and strong materials, such as gold, silver and crystal. The cup is made of a material that does not absorb liquid.

CHASUBLE

This is the outer garment worn by the priest celebrating Mass. It looks like a poncho, and comes in different colors that correspond to Holy Days or liturgical seasons.

CIBORIUM

When hosts are used during Mass, a ciborium holds the hosts distributed at Communion. It looks like a chalice with a lid, and is made of a valued and strong material.

COMMUNION CUP

See chalice.

COMMUNION PLATE

This plate holds the bread that is distributed during Communion.

CORPORAL

The corporal is a square piece of cloth that the priest places beneath the chalice and bread during Mass to collect crumbs or spills. It is also used underneath the ciborium or pyx when they are in the tabernacle.

CROSS

The cross is the main symbol of Christian faith, because Jesus Christ died on the cross. You will see crosses on top of Catholic and other Christian churches. Making the sign of the cross expresses faith in Christ.

GAUDETE SUNDAY

Priests can choose to wear a rose-colored chasuble on Gaudete Sunday, the third Sunday of Advent.

HOLY WATER FONT

This is a container for holy water that Catholics place at the entrance of their churches. People entering the church dip their fingers into the water of the font and bless themselves with the sign of the cross. Some churches use their baptismal font as the holy water font.

HOST

A host is a flat round piece of unleavened bread sometimes used as eucharistic bread.

LAETARE SUNDAY

Priests can choose to wear a rose-colored chasuble on Laetare Sunday, the fourth Sunday of Lent.

LECTERN

The lectern (or ambo) is a tall standing desk for preaching and reading. It holds the books from which the Scriptures are read during Mass. The readings, Gospel, and homily are usually delivered at the lectern.

LECTIONARY

The lectionary is a book and it contains all the scripture readings, including the Gospels, that are needed for Mass.

LITURGY of the EUCHARIST

This is the second part of Mass, and includes: the Presentation of the Gifts, the Eucharistic Prayer, the Great Amen, the Our Father and the Communion Rite.

LITURGY of the WORD

This is the first part of Mass, and includes: the First Reading, the Psalms, the Second Reading, the Alleluia, the Gospel, the Homily, the Creed and the Prayer of the Faithful.

PEW

A pew is a long bench that people use for sitting and kneeling in church.

PIPE ORGAN or PIANO

Many churches have a pipe organ or piano. One of the church members plays it during Mass because music is part of our celebration.

PRESIDER'S CHAIR

The chief presider at Mass sits in this chair during the prayer time after Communion and sometimes when other church members assist him in leading Mass.

PURIFICATOR

The priest uses a purificator, a linen cloth, to clean the vessels used during Communion.

PYX

The pyx is a flat metal container used to carry Communion to the sick.

RECONCILIATION ROOM

A room where Catholics confess any sins to the priest and receive forgiveness from God.

ROMAN COLLAR

A stiffly starched band of white linen cloth that priests attach to the front of their shirt collars.

SACRAMENTARY

The sacramentary is a book of prayers used during the Mass. It does not contain biblical readings, which are in the lectionary.

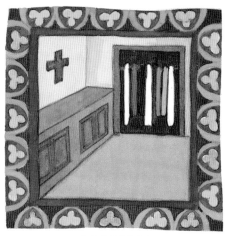

SACRISTY

A room where vestments, church furnishings and sacred vessels are kept and where the clergy and other ministers prepare for Mass.

SANCTUARY

The area in the church where the priest and other ministers lead prayers or celebrate Mass. It is also where the main altar in the church stands, and is emphasized by a decorative or raised floor.

SANCTUARY LAMP

This lamp hangs in the sanctuary. When it is burning, eucharistic bread is in the tabernacle.

SURPLICE

A loose white vestment worn over the cassock.

STOLE

A long, narrow cloth worn by priests and other clergy. It is draped around the neck. It symbolizes the authority that the church vests in its ministers.

TABERNACLE

The tabernacle is a special box where the eucharistic bread is kept between Masses. Tabernacles are unbreakable, immovable and dignified. They are usually located either in the sanctuary or in a side chapel.